AF323992

Bret Harte, from a photograph taken in New York,

Bret Harte Pocket Series No. 4

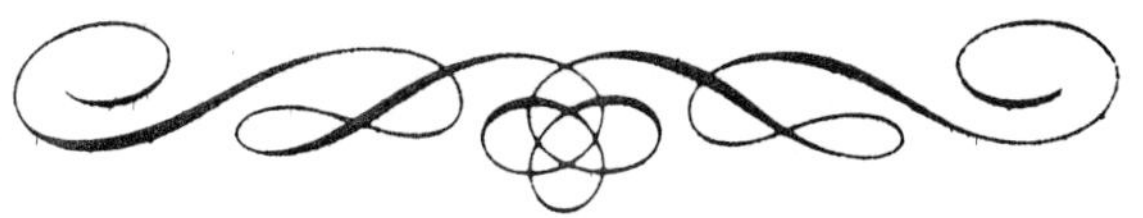

How Santa Claus Came To Simpson's Bar.

and

The Xmas Gift To Rupert.

by

Bret Harte

Star Rover House
Oakland, California

HOW SANTA CLAUS CAME TO SIMPSON'S BAR.

IT had been raining in the valley of the Sacramento. The North Fork had overflowed its banks and Rattlesnake Creek was impassable. The few boulders that had marked the summer ford at Simpson's Crossing were obliterated by a vast sheet of water stretching to the foothills. The up stage was stopped at Grangers; the last mail had been abandoned in the *tules*, the rider swimming for his life. "An area," remarked the "Sierra

Avalanche," with pensive local pride, " as large as the State of Massachusetts is now under water."

Nor was the weather any better in the foothills. The mud lay deep on the mountain road ; wagons that neither physical force nor moral objurgation could move from the evil ways into which they had fallen, encumbered the track, and the way to Simpson's Bar was indicated by broken-down teams and hard swearing. And farther on, cut off and inaccessible, rained upon and bedraggled, smitten by high winds and threatened by high water, Simpson's Bar, on the eve of Christmas day, 1862, clung like a swallow's nest to the rocky entablature and splintered capitals of Table Mountain, and shook in the blast.

As night shut down on the settlement, a few lights gleamed through the mist from the windows of cabins on either side of the highway now crossed and gullied by lawless streams and swept by marauding winds. Happily most of the population were gathered at Thompson's store, clustered around a red-hot stove, at which they silently spat in some accepted sense of social communion that perhaps rendered conversation unnecessary. Indeed, most methods of diversion had long since been exhausted on Simpson's Bar; high water had suspended the regular occupations on gulch and on river, and a consequent lack of money and whiskey had taken the zest from most illegitimate recreation. Even Mr. Hamlin was fain to leave the Bar with fifty dollars in his pocket, — the only amount actually realized of the large·sums won by him in the successful exercise of his arduous profession. "Ef I was asked," he remarked somewhat later, — "ef I was asked to pint out a purty little village where a retired sport as did n't care for money could exercise hisself, frequent and lively, I 'd say Simpson's Bar; but for a young man with a large family depending on his exertions, it don't pay." As Mr. Hamlin's family consisted mainly of female adults, this remark is quoted rather to show the breadth of his humor than the exact extent of his responsibilities.

Howbeit, the unconscious objects of this. satire sat that evening in the listless apathy begotten of idleness and lack of excitement. Even the sudden

6

splashing of hoofs before the door did not arouse
them. Dick Bullen alone paused in the act of
scraping out his pipe, and lifted his head, but no
other one of the group indicated any interest in,
or recognition of, the man who entered.

It was a figure familiar enough to the company,
and known in Simpson's Bar as " The Old Man."
A man of perhaps fifty years ; grizzled and scant
of hair, but still fresh and youthful of complexion.
A face full of ready, but not very powerful sympathy, with a chameleon-like aptitude for taking
on the shade and color of contiguous moods and
feelings. He had evidently just left some hilarious companions, and did not at first notice the
gravity of the group, but clapped the shoulder of
the nearest man jocularly, and threw himself into
a vacant chair.

" Jest heard the best thing out, boys ! Ye know
Smiley, over yar, — Jim Smiley, — funniest man
in the Bar ? Well, Jim was jest telling the richest
yarn about — "

" Smiley 's a —— fool," interrupted a gloomy
voice.

"A particular —— skunk," added another in sepulchral accents.

A silence followed these positive statements. The Old Man glanced quickly around the group. Then his face slowly changed. "That's so," he said reflectively, after a pause, "certingly a sort of a skunk and suthin of a fool. In course." He was silent for a moment as in painful contemplation of the unsavoriness and folly of the unpopular Smiley. "Dismal weather, ain't it?" he added, now fully embarked on the current of prevailing sentiment. "Mighty rough papers on the boys, and no show for money this season. And to-morrow's Christmas."

There was a movement among the men at this announcement, but whether of satisfaction or disgust was not plain. "Yes," continued the Old Man in the lugubrious tone he had, within the last few moments, unconsciously adopted, — "yes, Christmas, and to-night's Christmas eve. Ye see, boys, I kinder thought — that is, I sorter had an idee, jest passin' like, you know — that may be ye'd all like to come over to my house to-night and have a sort of tear round. But I suppose, now, you would n't? Don't feel like it, may be?" he added with anxious sympathy, peering into the faces of his companions.

"Well, I don't know," responded Tom Flynn with some cheerfulness. "P'r'aps we may. But how about your wife, Old Man? What does *she* say to it?"

The Old Man hesitated. His conjugal experience had not been a happy one, and the fact was known to Simpson's Bar. His first wife, a delicate, pretty little woman, had suffered keenly and secretly from the jealous suspicions of her husband, until one day he invited the whole Bar to his house to expose her infidelity. On arriving, the party found the shy, *petite* creature quietly engaged in her household duties, and retired abashed and discomfited. But the sensitive woman did not easily recover from the shock of this extraordinary outrage. It was with difficulty she regained her equanimity sufficiently to release her lover from the closet in which he was concealed and escape with him. She left a boy of three years to comfort her bereaved husband. The Old Man's present wife had been his cook. She was large, loyal, and aggressive.

Before he could reply, Joe Dimmick suggested with great directness that it was the " Old Man's house," and that, invoking the Divine Power, if the case were his own, he would invite whom he pleased, even if in so doing he imperilled his salvation. The Powers of Evil, he further remarked, should contend against him vainly. All this delivered with a terseness and vigor lost in this necessary translation.

" In course. Certainly. Thet 's it," said the Old Man with a sympathetic frown. " Thar 's no trouble about *thet*. It 's my own house, built every stick on it myself. Don't you be afeard o' her, boys. She *may* cut up a trifle rough, — ez wimmin do, — but she 'll come round." Secretly the Old Man trusted to the exaltation of liquor and the power of courageous example to sustain him in such an emergency.

As yet, Dick Bullen, the oracle and leader of Simpson's Bar, had not spoken. He now took his pipe from his lips. "Old Man, how 's that yer Johnny gettin' on ? Seems to me he did n't look so peart last time I seed him on the bluff heavin' rocks at Chinamen. Did n't seem to take much interest in it. Thar was a gang of 'em by yar yesterday, — drownded out up the river, — and I kinder thought o' Johnny, and how he 'd miss 'em ! May be now, we 'd be in the way ef he wus sick ?"

The father, evidently touched not only by this pathetic picture of Johnny's deprivation, but by the considerate delicacy of the speaker, hastened to assure him that Johnny was better and that a "little fun might 'liven him up." Whereupon Dick arose, shook himself, and saying, " I 'm ready. Lead the way, Old Man: here goes," himself led the way with a leap, a characteristic howl, and darted out into the night. As he passed through the outer room he caught up a blazing brand from the hearth. The action was repeated by the rest of the party, closely following and elbowing each other, and before the astonished proprietor of Thompson's grocery was aware of the intention of his guests, the room was deserted.

The night was pitchy dark. In the first gust of wind their temporary torches were extinguished, and only the red brands dancing and flitting in the gloom like drunken will-o'-the-wisps indicated their whereabouts. Their way led up Pine-Tree Cañon, at the head of which a broad, low, bark-thatched cabin burrowed in the mountain-side. It was the home of the Old Man, and the entrance to the tunnel in which he worked when he worked at all. Here the crowd paused for a moment, out of delicate deference to their host, who came up panting in the rear.

"P'r'aps ye 'd better hold on a second out yer, whilst I go in and see thet things is all right," said the Old Man, with an indifference he was far from feeling. The suggestion was graciously accepted, the door opened and closed on the host, and the crowd, leaning their backs against the wall and cowering under the eaves, waited and listened.

For a few moments there was no sound but the dripping of water from the eaves, and the stir and rustle of wrestling boughs above them. Then the men became uneasy, and whispered suggestion and suspicion passed from the one to the other. "Reckon she's caved in his head the first lick!" "Decoyed him inter the tunnel and barred him up, likely." "Got him down and sittin' on him." "Prob'ly bilin suthin to heave on us : stand clear the door, boys!" For just then the latch clicked, the door slowly opened, and a voice said, "Come in out o' the wet."

The voice was neither that of the Old Man nor of his wife. It was the voice of a small boy, its weak treble broken by that preternatural hoarseness which only vagabondage and the habit of premature self-assertion can give. It was the face of a small boy that looked up at theirs, — a face that might have been pretty and even refined but that it was darkened by evil knowledge from within, and dirt and hard experience from without. He had a blanket around his shoulders and had evidently just risen from his bed. "Come in," he repeated, "and don't make no noise. The Old Man's in there talking to mar," he continued, pointing to an adjacent room which seemed to be a kitchen, from which the Old Man's voice came in deprecating accents. "Let me be," he added, querulously, to Dick Bullen, who had caught him up, blanket and all, and was affecting to toss him into the fire, "let go o' me, you d—d old fool, d' ye hear?"

Thus adjured, Dick Bullen lowered Johnny to the ground with a smothered laugh, while the men, entering quietly, ranged themselves around a long table of rough boards which occupied the centre of the room. Johnny then gravely proceeded to a cupboard and brought out several articles which he deposited on the table. "Thar's whiskey. And crackers. And red herons. And cheese." He took a bite of the latter on his way to the table. "And sugar." He scooped up a mouthful *en route* with a small and very dirty hand. "And terbacker. Thar's dried appils too on the shelf, but I don't admire 'em. Appils is swellin'. Thar," he concluded, "now wade in, and don't be afeard. *I* don't mind the old woman. She don't b'long to *me*. S'long."

He had stepped to the threshold of a small room, scarcely larger than a closet, partitioned off from the main apartment, and holding in its dim recess a small bed. He stood there a moment looking at the company, his bare feet peeping from the blanket, and nodded.

"Hello, Johnny! You ain't goin' to turn in agin, are ye?" said Dick.

"Yes, I are," responded Johnny, decidedly.

"Why, wot 's up, old fellow?"

"I 'm sick."

"How sick?"

"I 've got a fevier. And childblains. And roomatiz," returned Johnny, and vanished within. After a moment's pause, he added in the dark, apparently from under the bedclothes, — "And biles!"

There was an embarrassing silence. The men looked at each other, and at the fire. Even with the appetizing banquet before them, it seemed as if they might again fall into the despondency of Thompson's grocery, when the voice of the Old Man, incautiously lifted, came deprecatingly from the kitchen.

"Certainly! Thet 's so. In course they is. A gang o' lazy drunken loafers, and that ar Dick

Bullen 's the ornariest of all.   Did n't hev no more *sabe* than to come round yar with sickness in the house and no provision.   Thet 's what I said : ' Bullen,' sez I, ' it 's crazy drunk you are, or a fool,' sez I, ' to think o' such a thing.'   'Staples,' I sez, ' be you a man, Staples, and 'spect to raise h—ll under my roof and invalids lyin' round ?' But they would come, — they would.   Thet 's wot you must 'spect o' such trash as lays round the Bar."

A burst of laughter from the men followed this unfortunate exposure.   Whether it was overheard in the kitchen, or whether the Old Man's irate companion had just then exhausted all other modes of expressing her contemptuous indignation, I cannot say, but a back door was suddenly slammed with great violence.   A moment later and the Old Man reappeared, haply unconscious of the cause of the late hilarious outburst, and smiled blandly.

"The old woman thought she 'd jest run over to Mrs McFadden's for a sociable call," he explained, with jaunty indifference, as he took a seat at the board.

Oddly enough it needed this untoward incident to relieve the embarrassment that was beginning to be felt by the party, and their natural audacity returned with their host. I do not propose to record the convivialities of that evening. The inquisitive reader will accept the statement that the conversation was characterized by the same intellectual exaltation, the same cautious reverence, the same fastidious delicacy, the same rhetorical precision, and the same logical and coherent discourse somewhat later in the evening, which distinguish similar gatherings of the masculine sex in more civilized localities and under more favorable auspices. No glasses were broken in the absence of any; no liquor was uselessly spilt on floor or table in the scarcity of that article.

It was nearly midnight when the festivities were interrupted. "Hush," said Dick Bullen, holding up his hand. It was the querulous voice of Johnny from his adjacent closet: "O dad!"

The Old Man arose hurriedly and disappeared in the closet. Presently he reappeared. "His rheumatiz is coming on agin bad," he explained, "and he wants rubbin'." He lifted the demijohn of whiskey from the table and shook it. It was empty. Dick Bullen put down his tin cup with an embarrassed laugh. So did the others. The Old Man examined their contents and said hopefully, "I reckon that's enough; he don't need much. You hold on all o' you for a spell, and I'll be back"; and vanished in the closet with an old flannel shirt and the whiskey. The door closed but imperfectly, and the following dialogue was distinctly audible :—

"Now, sonny, whar does she ache worst?"

"Sometimes over yar and sometimes under yer; but it's most powerful from yer to yer. Rub yer, dad."

A silence seemed to indicate a brisk rubbing. Then Johnny :

"Hevin' a good time out yer, dad?"

"Yes, sonny."

"To-morrer's Chrismiss, — ain't it?"

"Yes, sonny. How does she feel now?"

"Better. Rub a little furder down. Wot's Chrismiss, anyway? Wot's it all about?"

"O, it's a day."

This exhaustive definition was apparently satisfactory, for there was a silent interval of rubbing. Presently Johnny again:

"Mar sez that everywhere else but yer everybody gives things to everybody Chrismiss, and then she jist waded inter you. She sez thar's a man they call Sandy Claws, not a white man, you know, but a kind o' Chinemin, comes down the chimbley night afore Chrismiss and gives things to chillern,—boys like me. Puts 'em in their butes! Thet's what she tried to play upon me. Easy now, pop, whar are you rubbin' to,—thet's a mile from the place. She jest made that up, did n't she, jest to aggrewate me and you? Don't rub thar. . . . . Why, dad!"

In the great quiet that seemed to have fallen upon the house the sigh of the near pines and the drip of leaves without was very distinct. Johnny's voice, too, was lowered as he went on, "Don't you take on now, fur I 'm gettin' all right fast. Wot 's the boys doin' out thar?"

The Old Man partly opened the door and peered through. His guests were sitting there sociably enough, and there were a few silver coins and a lean buckskin purse on the table. "Bettin' on suthin, — some little game or 'nother. They 're all right," he replied to Johnny, and recommenced his rubbing.

"I 'd like to take a hand and win some money," said Johnny, reflectively, after a pause.

The Old Man glibly repeated what was evidently a familiar formula, that if Johnny would wait until he struck it rich in the tunnel he 'd have lots of money, etc., etc.

"Yes," said Johnny, "but you don't. And whether you strike it or I win it, it 's about the same. It 's all luck. But it 's mighty cur'o's about Chrismiss, — ain't it ? Why do they call it Chrismiss ? "

Perhaps from some instinctive deference to the overhearing of his guests, or from some vague sense of incongruity, the Old Man's reply was so low as to be inaudible beyond the room.

"Yes," said Johnny, with some slight abatement of interest, "I 've heerd o' *him* before. Thar, that 'll do, dad. I don't ache near so bad as I did.

Now wrap me tight in this yer blanket. So. Now," he added in a muffled whisper, "sit down yer by me till I go asleep." To assure himself of obedience, he disengaged one hand from the blanket and, grasping his father's sleeve, again composed himself to rest.

For some moments the Old Man waited patiently. Then the unwonted stillness of the house excited his curiosity, and without moving from the bed, he cautiously opened the door with his disengaged hand, and looked into the main room. To his infinite surprise it was dark and deserted. But even then a smouldering log on the hearth broke, and by the upspringing blaze he saw the figure of Dick Bullen sitting by the dying embers.

"Hello!"

Dick started, rose, and came somewhat unsteadily toward him.

"Whar 's the boys ?" said the Old Man.

"Gone up the cañon on a little *pasear*. They 're coming back for me in a minit. I 'm waitin' round for 'em. What are you starin' at, Old Man?" he added with a forced laugh ; "do you think I 'm drunk ?"

The Old Man might have been pardoned the supposition, for Dick's eyes were humid and his face flushed. He loitered and lounged back to the chimney, yawned, shook himself, buttoned up his coat and laughed. "Liquor ain't so plenty as that, Old Man. Now don't you git up," he continued, as the Old Man made a movement to release his sleeve from Johnny's hand. "Don't you mind manners. Sit jest whar you be; I 'm goin' in a jiffy. Thar, that 's them now."

There was a low tap at the door. Dick Bullen opened it quickly, nodded "Good night" to his host, and disappeared. The Old Man would have followed him but for the hand that still unconsciously grasped his sleeve. He could have easily disengaged it: it was small, weak, and emaciated. But perhaps because it *was* small, weak, and emaciated, he changed his mind, and, drawing his chair closer to the bed, rested his head upon it. In this defenceless attitude the potency of his earlier potations surprised him. The room flickered and faded before his eyes, reappeared, faded again, went out, and left him — asleep.

Meantime Dick Bullen, closing the door, confronted his companions. "Are you ready?" said Staples. "Ready," said Dick; "what's the time?" "Past twelve," was the reply; "can you make it? — it's nigh on fifty miles, the round trip hither and yon." "I reckon," returned Dick, shortly. "Whar's the mare?" "Bill and Jack's holdin' her at the crossin'." "Let 'em hold on a minit longer," said Dick.

He turned and re-entered the house softly. By the light of the guttering candle and dying fire he saw that the door of the little room was open. He stepped toward it on tiptoe and looked in. The Old Man had fallen back in his chair, snoring, his helpless feet thrust out in a line with his collapsed shoulders, and his hat pulled over his eyes. Beside him, on a narrow wooden bedstead, lay Johnny, muffled tightly in a blanket that hid all save a strip of forehead and a few curls damp with perspiration. Dick Bullen made a step forward, hesitated, and glanced over his shoulder into the deserted room. Everything was quiet. With a sudden resolution he parted his huge mustaches with both hands and stooped over the sleeping boy. But even as he did so a mischievous blast, lying in wait, swooped down the chimney, rekindled the hearth, and lit up the room with a shameless glow from which Dick fled in bashful terror.

His companions were already waiting for him at the crossing. Two of them were struggling in the darkness with some strange misshapen bulk, which as Dick came nearer took the semblance of a great yellow horse.

It was the mare. She was not a pretty picture. From her Roman nose to her rising haunches, from her arched spine hidden by the stiff *machillas* of a Mexican saddle, to her thick, straight, bony legs, there was not a line of equine grace. In her half-blind but wholly vicious white eyes, in her protruding under lip, in her monstrous color, there was nothing but ugliness and vice.

"Now then," said Staples, "stand cl'ar of her heels, boys, and up with you. Don't miss your first holt of her mane, and mind ye get your off stirrup *quick*. Ready!"

There was a leap, a scrambling struggle, a bound, a wild retreat of the crowd, a circle of flying hoofs, two springless leaps that jarred the earth, a rapid play and jingle of spurs, a plunge, and then the voice of Dick somewhere in the darkness, " All right ! "

" Don't take the lower road back onless you 're hard pushed for time ! Don't hold her in down hill ! We 'll be at the ford at five. G' lang ! Hoopa ! Mula ! GO ! "

A splash, a spark struck from the ledge in the road, a clatter in the rocky cut beyond, and Dick was gone.

    .   .   .   .   .

Sing, O Muse, the ride of Richard Bullen ! Sing, O Muse of chivalrous men ! the sacred quest, the doughty deeds, the battery of low churls, the fearsome ride and grewsome perils of the Flower of Simpson's Bar ! Alack ! she is dainty, this Muse ! She will have none of this bucking brute and swaggering, ragged rider, and I must fain follow him in prose, afoot !

It was one o'clock, and yet he had only gained

Rattlesnake Hill. For in that time Jovita had re-
hearsed to him all her imperfections and practised
all her vices. Thrice had she stumbled. Twice
had she thrown up her Roman nose in a straight
line with the reins, and, resisting bit and spur,
struck out madly across country. Twice had she
reared, and, rearing, fallen backward; and twice
had the agile Dick, unharmed, regained his seat
before she found her vicious legs again. And a
mile beyond them, at the foot of a long hill, was
Rattlesnake Creek. Dick knew that here was the
crucial test of his ability to perform his enterprise,
set his teeth grimly, put his knees well into her
flanks, and changed his defensive tactics to brisk
aggression. Bullied and maddened, Jovita began
the descent of the hill. Here the artful Richard
pretended to hold her in with ostentatious objurgation and well-feigned cries of alarm. It is unnecessary to add that Jovita instantly ran away.
Nor need I state the time made in the descent; it
is written in the chronicles of Simpson's Bar.
Enough that in another moment, as it seemed to
Dick, she was splashing on the overflowed banks

of Rattlesnake Creek. As Dick expected, the momentum she had acquired carried her beyond the point of balking, and, holding her well together for a mighty leap, they dashed into the middle of the swiftly flowing current. A few moments of kicking, wading, and swimming, and Dick drew a long breath on the opposite bank.

The road from Rattlesnake Creek to Red Mountain was tolerably level. Either the plunge in Rattlesnake Creek had dampened her baleful fire, or the art which led to it had shown her the superior wickedness of her rider, for Jovita no longer wasted her surplus energy in wanton conceits. Once she bucked, but it was from force of habit; once she shied, but it was from a new freshly painted meeting-house at the crossing of the county road. Hollows, ditches, gravelly deposits, patches of freshly springing grasses, flew from beneath her rattling hoofs. She began to smell unpleasantly, once or twice she coughed slightly, but there was no abatement of her strength or speed. By two o'clock he had passed Red Mountain and begun the descent to the plain. Ten minutes later the driver of the fast Pioneer coach was overtaken and passed by a "man on a Pinto hoss," — an event sufficiently notable for remark. At half past two Dick rose in his stirrups with a great shout. Stars were glittering through the rifted clouds, and beyond him, out of the plain, rose two spires, a flagstaff, and a straggling line of black objects. Dick jingled his spurs and swung his *riata*, Jovita bounded forward, and in another moment they swept into Tuttleville and drew up before the wooden piazza of "The Hotel of All Nations."

What transpired that night at Tuttleville is not strictly a part of this record. Briefly I may state, however, that after Jovita had been handed over to a sleepy ostler, whom she at once kicked into unpleasant consciousness, Dick sallied out with the bar-keeper for a tour of the sleeping town. Lights still gleamed from a few saloons and gambling-houses; but, avoiding these, they stopped before several closed shops, and by persistent tapping and judicious outcry roused the proprietors from their beds, and made them unbar the doors of their magazines and expose their wares. Sometimes they were met by curses, but oftener by interest and some concern in their needs, and the interview was invariably concluded by a drink. It was three o'clock before this pleasantry was given over, and with a small waterproof bag of india-rubber strapped on his shoulders Dick returned to the hotel. But here he was waylaid by Beauty, — Beauty opulent in charms, affluent in dress, persuasive in speech, and Spanish in accent! In vain she repeated the invitation in "Excelsior," happily scorned by all Alpine-climbing youth, and rejected by this child of the Sierras, — a rejection softened in this instance by a laugh and his last gold coin. And then he sprang to the saddle and dashed down the lonely street and out into the lonelier plain, where presently the lights, the black line of houses, the spires, and the flagstaff sank into the earth behind him again and were lost in the distance.

The storm had cleared away, the air was brisk and cold, the outlines of adjacent landmarks were distinct, but it was half past four before Dick reached the meeting-house and the crossing of the county road. To avoid the rising grade he had taken a longer and more circuitous road, in whose viscid mud Jovita sank fetlock deep at every bound. It was a poor preparation for a steady ascent of five miles more; but Jovita, gathering her legs under her, took it with her usual blind, unreasoning fury, and a half-hour later reached the long level that led to Rattlesnake Creek. Another half-hour would bring him to the creek. He threw the reins lightly upon the neck of the mare, chirruped to her, and began to sing.

Suddenly Jovita shied with a bound that would have unseated a less practised rider. Hanging to her rein was a figure that had leaped from the bank, and at the same time from the road before her arose a shadowy horse and rider. "Throw up your hands," commanded this second apparition, with an oath.

Dick felt the mare tremble, quiver, and apparently sink under him. He knew what it meant and was prepared.

"Stand aside, Jack Simpson, I know you, you d—d thief. Let me pass or — "

He did not finish the sentence. Jovita rose straight in the air with a terrific bound, throwing the figure from her bit with a single shake of her vicious head, and charged with deadly malevolence down on the impediment before her. An oath, a pistol-shot, horse and highwayman rolled over in the road, and the next moment Jovita was a hundred yards away. But the good right arm of her rider, shattered by a bullet, dropped helplessly at his side.

Without slacking his speed he shifted the reins to his left hand. But a few moments later he was obliged to halt and tighten the saddle-girths that had slipped in the onset. This in his crippled condition took some time. He had no fear of pursuit, but looking up he saw that the eastern stars were already paling, and that the distant peaks had lost their ghostly whiteness, and now stood out blackly against a lighter sky. Day was upon him. Then completely absorbed in a single idea, he forgot the pain of his wound, and mounting again dashed on toward Rattlesnake Creek.

But now Jovita's breath came broken by gasps, Dick reeled in his saddle, and brighter and brighter grew the sky.

Ride, Richard; run, Jovita; linger, O day!

For the last few rods there was a roaring in his ears. Was it exhaustion from loss of blood, or what? He was dazed and giddy as he swept down the hill, and did not recognize his surroundings. Had he taken the wrong road, or was this Rattlesnake Creek?

It was. But the brawling creek he had swam a few hours before had risen, more than doubled its volume, and now rolled a swift and resistless river between him and Rattlesnake Hill. For the first time that night Richard's heart sank within him. The river, the mountain, the quickening east, swam before his eyes. He shut them to recover his self-control. In that brief interval, by some fantastic mental process, the little room at Simpson's Bar and the figures of the sleeping father and son rose upon him. He opened his eyes wildly, cast off his coat, pistol, boots, and saddle, bound his precious pack tightly to his shoulders, grasped the bare flanks of Jovita with his bared knees, and with a shout dashed into the yellow water. A cry rose from the opposite bank as the head of a man and horse struggled for a few moments against the battling current, and then were swept away amidst uprooted trees and whirling drift-wood.

.   .   .   .   .

The Old Man started and woke. The fire on the hearth was dead, the candle in the outer room flickering in its socket, and somebody was rapping at the door. He opened it, but fell back with a cry before the dripping, half-naked figure that reeled against the doorpost.

"Dick?"

"Hush! Is he awake yet?"

"No, — but, Dick? — "

"Dry up, you old fool! Get me some whiskey *quick!*" The Old Man flew and returned with — an empty bottle! Dick would have sworn, but his strength was not equal to the occasion. He staggered, caught at the handle of the door, and motioned to the Old Man.

"Thar's suthin' in my pack yer for Johnny. Take it off. I can't."

The Old Man unstrapped the pack and laid it before the exhausted man.

"Open it, quick!"

He did so with trembling fingers. It contained only a few poor toys, — cheap and barbaric enough, goodness knows, but bright with paint and tinsel. One of them was broken; another, I fear, was irretrievably ruined by water; and on the third — ah me! there was a cruel spot.

"It don't look like much, that's a fact," said Dick, ruefully. . . . . . "But it's the best we could do. . . . . Take 'em, Old Man, and put 'em in his stocking, and tell him — tell him, you know — hold me, Old Man —" The Old Man caught at his sinking figure. "Tell him," said Dick, with a weak little laugh, — "tell him Sandy Claus has come."

And even so, bedraggled, ragged, unshaven, and unshorn, with one arm hanging helplessly at his side, Santa Claus came to Simpson's Bar and fell

34

fainting on the first threshold. The Christmas
dawn came slowly after, touching the remoter
peaks with the rosy warmth of ineffable love.
And it looked so tenderly on Simpson's Bar that
the whole mountain, as if caught in a generous
action, blushed to the skies.

THE CHRISTMAS GIFT THAT CAME TO RUPERT.

A STORY FOR LITTLE SOLDIERS.

IT was the Christmas season in California, — a season of falling rain and springing grasses. There were intervals when, through driving clouds and flying scud, the sun visited the haggard hills with a miracle, and death and resurrection were as one, and out of the very throes of decay a joyous life struggled outward and upward. Even the storms that swept down the dead leaves nurtured the tender buds that took their places. There were no episodes of snowy silence ; over the quickening fields the farmer's ploughshare hard followed the furrows left by the latest rains. Perhaps it was for this reason that the Christmas evergreens which decorated the drawing-room took upon themselves a foreign aspect, and offered a weird contrast to the roses, seen dimly through the windows, as the southwest wind beat their soft faces against the panes.

" Now," said the Doctor, drawing his chair closer to the fire, and looking mildly but firmly at the semicircle of flaxen heads around him, " I want it distinctly understood before I begin my story, that I am not to be interrupted by any ridiculous questions. At the first one I shall stop. At the second, I shall feel it my duty to administer a dose of castor-oil, all around. The boy that moves his legs or arms will be understood to invite amputation. I have brought my instruments with me, and never allow pleasure to interfere with my business. Do you promise ? "

"Yes, sir," said six small voices, simultaneously. The volley was, however, followed by half a dozen dropping questions.

"Silence! Bob, put your feet down, and stop rattling that sword. Flora shall sit by my side, like a little lady, and be an example to the rest. Fung Tang shall stay, too, if he likes. Now, turn down the gas a little; there, that will do, — just enough to make the fire look brighter, and to show off the Christmas candles. Silence, everybody! The boy who cracks an almond, or breathes too loud over his raisins, will be put out of the room."

There was a profound silence. Bob laid his sword tenderly aside, and nursed his leg thoughtfully. Flora, after coquettishly adjusting the pocket of her little apron, put her arm upon the Doctor's shoulder, and permitted herself to be drawn beside him. Fung Tang, the little heathen page, who was permitted, on this rare occasion, to share the Christian revels in the drawing-room, surveyed the group with a smile that was at once sweet and philosophical. The light ticking of a French clock on the mantel, supported by a young shepherdess of bronze complexion and great symmetry of limb, was the only sound that disturbed the Christmas-like peace of the apartment, — a peace which held the odors of evergreens, new toys, cedar-boxes, glue, and varnish in an harmonious combination that passed all understanding.

" About four years ago at this time," began the Doctor, " I attended a course of lectures in a certain city. One of the professors, who was a sociable, kindly man, — though somewhat practical and hard-headed, — invited me to his house on Christmas night. I was very glad to go, as I was anxious to see one of his sons, who, though only twelve years old, was said to be very clever. I dare not tell you how many Latin verses this little fellow could recite, or how many English ones he had composed. In the first place, you 'd want me to repeat them; secondly, I 'm not a judge of poetry, Latin or English. But there were judges who said they were wonderful for a boy, and everybody predicted a splendid future for him. Everybody but his father. He shook his head doubtingly, whenever it was mentioned, for, as I have told you, he was a practical, matter-of-fact man.

"There was a pleasant party at the Professor's that night. All the children of the neighborhood were there, and among them the Professor's clever son, Rupert, as they called him, — a thin little chap, about as tall as Bobby there, and as fair and delicate as Flora by my side. His health was feeble, his father said; he seldom ran about and played with other boys, preferring to stay at home and brood over his books, and compose what he called his verses.

"Well, we had a Christmas-tree just like this, and we had been laughing and talking, calling off the names of the children who had presents on the tree, and everybody was very happy and joyous, when one of the children suddenly uttered a cry of mingled surprise and hilarity, and said, 'Here's something for Rupert; and what do you think it is?'

"We all guessed. 'A desk'; 'A copy of Milton'; 'A gold pen'; 'A rhyming dictionary.'

40

' No ? what then ? '

"' A drum !'

"' A what ?' asked everybody.

"' A drum ! with Rupert's name on it.'

"Sure enough there it was. A good-sized, bright, new, brass-bound drum, with a slip of paper on it, with the inscription, 'FOR RUPERT.'

"Of course we all laughed, and thought it a good joke. 'You see you're to make a noise in the world, Rupert!' said one. 'Here's parchment for the poet,' said another. 'Rupert's last work in sheepskin covers,' said a third. 'Give us a classical tune, Rupert,' said a fourth; and so on. But Rupert seemed too mortified to speak; he changed color, bit his lips, and finally burst into a passionate fit of crying, and left the room. Then those who had joked him felt ashamed, and everybody began to ask who had put the drum there. But no one knew, or if they did, the unexpected sympathy awakened for the sensitive boy kept them silent. Even the servants were called up and questioned, but no one could give any idea where it came from. And, what was still more singular, everybody declared that up to the moment it was produced, no one had seen it hanging on the tree. What do I think? Well, I have my own opinion. But no questions! Enough for you to know that Rupert did not come down stairs again that night, and the party soon after broke up.

"I had almost forgotten those things, for the war of the Rebellion broke out the next spring, and I was appointed surgeon in one of the new regiments, and was on my way to the seat of war. But I had to pass through the city where the Professor lived, and there I met him. My first question was about Rupert. The Professor shook his head sadly. 'He's not so well,' he said; 'he has been declining since last Christmas, when you saw him. A very strange case,' he added, giving it a long Latin name, — 'a very singular case. But go and see him yourself,' he urged; 'it may distract his mind and do him good.'

"I went accordingly to the Professor's house, and found Rupert lying on a sofa, propped up with pillows. Around him were scattered his books,

and, what seemed in singular contrast, that drum
I told you about was hanging on a nail, just above
his head. His face was thin and wasted; there
was a red spot on either cheek, and his eyes were
very bright and widely opened. He was glad to
see me, and when I told him where I was going,
he asked a thousand questions about the war. I
thought I had thoroughly diverted his mind from
its sick and languid fancies, when he suddenly
grasped my hand and drew me toward him.

"'Doctor,' said he, in a low whisper, 'you won't
laugh at me if I tell you something?'

"'No, certainly not,' I said.

"'You remember that drum?' he said, pointing
to the glittering toy that hung against the wall.
'You know, too, how it came to me. A few weeks
after Christmas, I was lying half asleep here, and
the drum was hanging on the wall, when suddenly
I heard it beaten; at first, low and slowly, then
faster and louder, until its rolling filled the house.
In the middle of the night, I heard it again. I

did not dare to tell anybody about it, but I have heard it every night ever since.'

"He paused and looked anxiously in my face. 'Sometimes,' he continued, 'it is played softly, sometimes loudly, but always quickening to a long-roll, so loud and alarming that I have looked to see people coming into my room to ask what was the matter. But I think, Doctor, — I think,' he repeated slowly, looking up with painful interest into my face, 'that no one hears it but myself.'

"I thought so, too, but I asked him if he had heard it at any other time.

"'Once or twice in the daytime,' he replied, 'when I have been reading or writing ; then very loudly, as though it were angry, and tried in that way to attract my attention away from my books.'

"I looked into his face, and placed my hand upon his pulse. His eyes were very bright, and his pulse a little flurried and quick. I then tried to explain to him that he was very weak, and that his senses were very acute, as most weak people's are ; and how that when he read, or grew interested and excited, or when he was tired at night, the throbbing of a big artery made the beating sound he heard. He listened to me with a sad smile of unbelief, but thanked me, and in a little while I went away. But as I was going down stairs, I met the Professor. I gave him my opinion of the case,— well, no matter what it was.

"'He wants fresh air and exercise,' said the Professor, 'and some practical experience of life, sir.' The Professor was not a bad man, but he was a little worried and impatient, and thought — as clever people are apt to think — that things which he did n't understand were either silly or improper.

"I left the city that very day, and in the excitement of battle-fields and hospitals, I forgot all about little Rupert, nor did I hear of him again, until one day, meeting an old classmate in the army, who had known the Professor, he told me that Rupert had become quite insane, and that in one of his paroxysms he had escaped from the house, and as he had never been found, it was feared that he had fallen in the river and was drowned. I was terribly shocked for the moment, as you may imagine; but, dear me, I was living just then among scenes as terrible and shocking, and I had little time to spare to mourn over poor Rupert.

" It was not long after receiving this intelligence that we had a terrible battle, in which a portion of our army was surprised and driven back with great slaughter. I was detached from my brigade to ride over to the battle-field and assist the surgeons of the beaten division, who had more on their hands than they could attend to. When I reached the barn that served for a temporary hospital, I went at once to work. Ah, Bob," said the Doctor, thoughtfully taking the bright sword from the hands of the half-frightened Bob, and holding it gravely before him, "these pretty playthings are symbols of cruel, ugly realities.

" I turned to a tall, stout Vermonter," he continued very slowly, tracing a pattern on the rug with the point of the scabbard, "who was badly wounded in both thighs, but he held up his hands and begged me to help others first who needed it more than he. I did not at first heed his request, for this kind of unselfishness was very common in the army; but he went on, 'For God's sake, Doctor, leave me here; there is a drummer-boy of our regiment — a mere child — dying, if he is n't dead now. Go, and see him first. He lies over there. He saved more than one life. He was at his post in the panic this morning, and saved the honor of the regiment.' I was so much more impressed by the man's manner than by the substance of his speech, which was, however, corroborated by the other poor fellows stretched around me, that I passed over to where the drummer lay, with his drum beside him. I gave one glance at his face —and — yes, Bob — yes, my children — it *was* Rupert.

"Well! well! it needed not the chalked cross which my brother-surgeons had left upon the rough board whereon he lay to show how urgent was the relief he sought; it needed not the prophetic words of the Vermonter, nor the damp that mingled with the brown curls that clung to his pale forehead, to show how hopeless it was now. I called him by name. He opened his eyes — larger, I thought, in the new vision that was beginning to dawn upon

him — and recognized me. He whispered, 'I'm glad you are come, but I don't think you can do me any good.'

"I could not tell him a lie. I could not say anything. I only pressed his hand in mine, as he went on.

"'But you will see father, and ask him to forgive me. Nobody is to blame but myself. It was a long time before I understood why the drum came to me that Christmas night, and why it kept calling to me every night, and what it said. I know it now. The work is done, and I am content. Tell father it is better as it is. I should have lived only to worry and perplex him, and something in me tells me this is right.'

"He lay still for a moment, and then, grasping my hand, said, —

"'Hark!'

"I listened, but heard nothing but the suppressed moans of the wounded men around me. 'The drum,' he said faintly; 'don't you hear it? The drum is calling me.'

"He reached out his arm to where it lay, as though he would embrace it.

"'Listen,' he went on, 'it's the reveille. There are the ranks drawn up in review. Don't you see the sunlight flash down the long line of bayonets? Their faces are shining, — they present arms, — there comes the General; but his face I cannot look at, for the glory round his head. He sees me; he smiles, it is —' And with a name upon his lips that he had learned long ago, he stretched himself wearily upon the planks, and lay quite still.

"That's all. No questions now; never mind what became of the drum. Who's that snivelling? Bless my soul, where's my pill-box?"

LIQUID COURT PLASTER

immediately dries, forming a tough, transparent, waterproof coating. "New-Skin" heals Cuts, Abrasions, Hang-Nails, Chapped and Split Lips or Fingers, Burns, Blisters, etc. Instantly relieves Chilblains, Frosted Ears, Stings of Insects, Chafed or Blistered Feet, Callous Spots, etc., etc.

A coating on the sensitive parts will protect the feet from being chafed or blistered by new or heavy shoes. MECHANICS, SPORTSMEN, BICYCLISTS, GOLFERS, in fact all of us, are liable to bruise, scratch or scrape our skin. "NEW-SKIN" will heal these injuries, will not wash off, and after it is applied the injury is forgotten as "NEW-SKIN" makes a temporary new skin until the broken skin is healed under it. "Paint it with "New-Skin" and forget it" is literally true.

CAUTION: WE GUARANTEE our claims for "NEW-SKIN". No one guarantees substitutes or imitations trading on our reputation, and the guarantee of an imitator would be worthless any way.

ALWAYS INSIST ON GETTING "NEW-SKIN".

Sample size, 10c. Family size (like illustration), 25c. Two ounce bottles (for surgeons and hospitals), 50c.

AT THE DRUGGISTS, or we will mail a package anywhere in the United States on receipt of price.

Douglas Mfg. Co. 64-66 Poplar Street, BROOKLYN, N.Y.

Dept. 139